D1386377

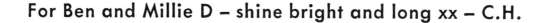

For Ben and Millie D – shine bright and long xx – C.H.

**For Will, Danni, Ellie, Liah and Kaufman.
The only way to experience interstellar travel
is with a dog in a rocket! – B.W.**

BLOOMSBURY CHILDREN'S BOOKS
Bloomsbury Publishing Plc
50 Bedford Square, London, WC1B 3DP, UK
BLOOMSBURY, BLOOMSBURY CHILDREN'S BOOKS and the Diana logo are trademarks of Bloomsbury Publishing Plc
First published in Great Britain by Bloomsbury Publishing Plc

A catalogue record for this book is available from the British Library

ISBN 978 1 4088 9299 2 (HB)
ISBN 978 1 4088 9298 5 (PB)
ISBN 978 1 4088 9300 5 (eBook)

3 5 7 9 10 8 6 4 2

Printed and bound in China by Leo Paper Products, Heshan, Guangdong
All papers used by Bloomsbury Publishing Plc are natural, recyclable products from wood grown in well managed forests.
The manufacturing processes conform to the environmental regulations of the country of origin.

To find out more about our authors and books visit www.bloomsbury.com and sign up for our newsletters

MEET THE PLANETS

Caryl Hart

Illustrated by **Bethan Woollvin**

BLOOMSBURY
CHILDREN'S BOOKS

LONDON OXFORD NEW YORK NEW DELHI SYDNEY

The sun shines so bright in the daytime
but when the **moon** comes out at **night**,
we see loads of beautiful twinkling stars
as we switch off the warm bedroom light.

It's ever so hard to imagine,
since **stars** really look kind of small,
that each one's a **planet**, a **sun** or a **moon** –
they're **not** shining **sequins** at all!

So . . .

Let's go on a fabulous journey
and meet **all** the planets up high.
It's too far to go in a car or a bus . . .

so we'll climb into a rocket
and fly!

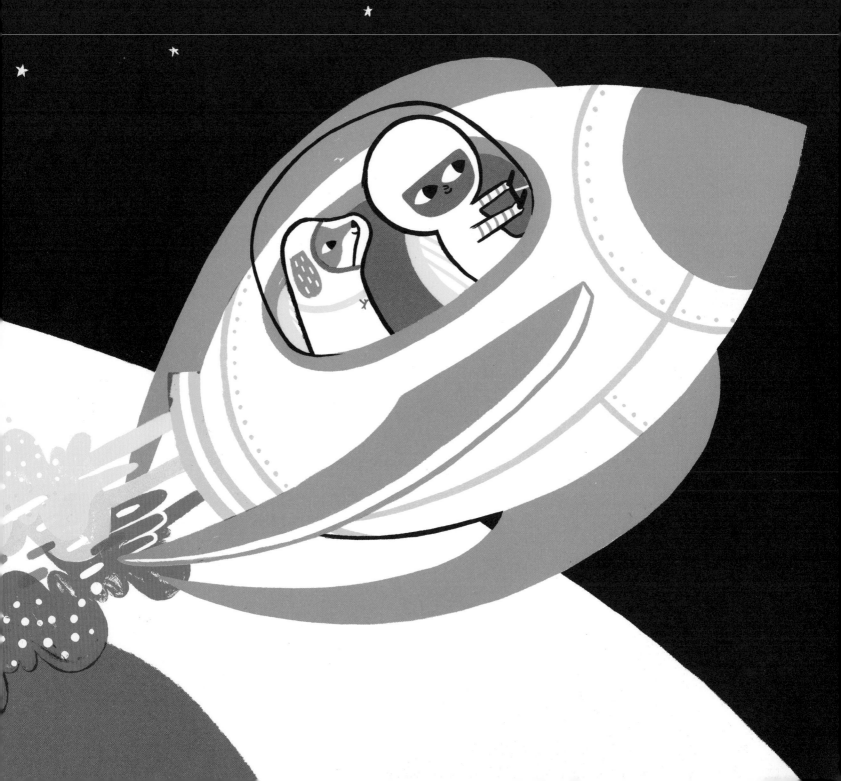

Hello, I'm **THE SUN** – nice to meet you!
I'm the **biggest** thing up in the sky.
I'm friendly but don't get **too close** now
or I'll **frizzle** you up to a fry!

My heat keeps you **warm** in the daytime.
My light helps plants grow wild and green.
But, be careful, I'm really a

great ball of fire –

the **HOTTEST** and **FIERCEST**
you've seen!

I'm **MERCURY** —
bet you can't CATCH me!
I zip round the sun at top speed.
At fifty kilometres per second —
I'm a very FAST planet indeed.

Wheeeeeeeeeeeeeeeee!

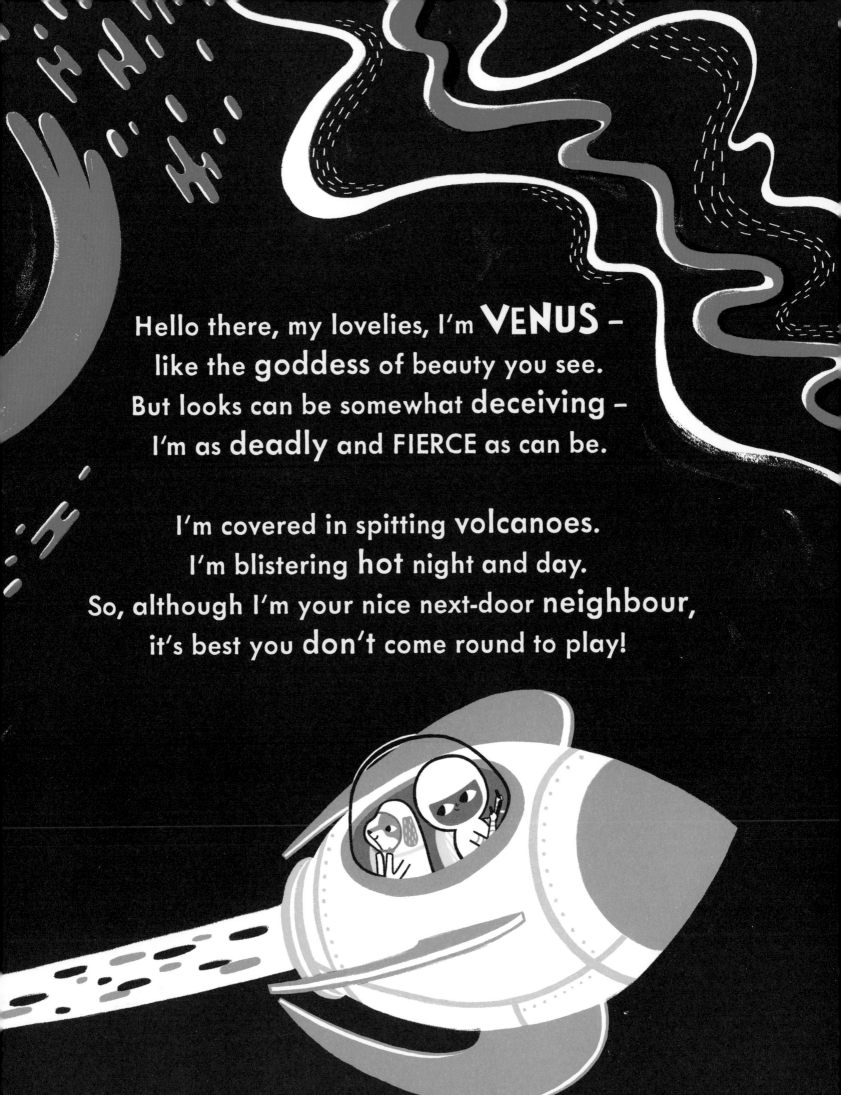

Hello there, my lovelies, I'm **VENUS** –
like the **goddess** of beauty you see.
But looks can be somewhat **deceiving** –
I'm as **deadly** and **FIERCE** as can be.

I'm covered in spitting **volcanoes**.
I'm blistering **hot** night and day.
So, although I'm your nice next-door **neighbour**,
it's best you **don't** come round to play!

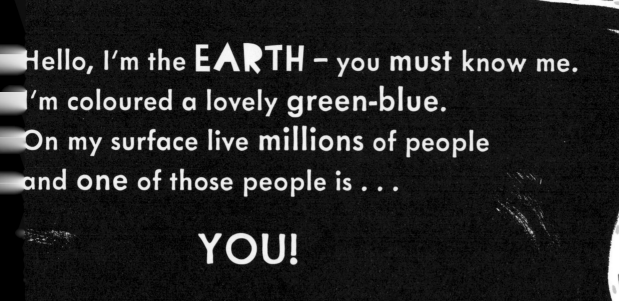

Hello, I'm the EARTH – you must know me.
I'm coloured a lovely green-blue.
On my surface live millions of people
and one of those people is . . .

YOU!

I have oceans and forests and mountains,
clean air and fresh water to drink.
There are no other planets quite like me
so you're LUCKY to have me, I think.

Shh! I'm the silver **MOON**, darling –
I keep **watch** while you're tucked up in bed.
But look upwards and sometimes you'll see me –
a ghost in broad **daylight** instead!

Howdy, I'm **MARS** – howya doin?
Most folk around here call me **RED**.
It's because of this rust-coloured dust
that these pesky winds blow round my head.

It's super **cold** here in the winter.
There's **NO** water or food – nope, just **ice**.
But climb my **volcano**, it's real super high,
and the view from up there is real nice.

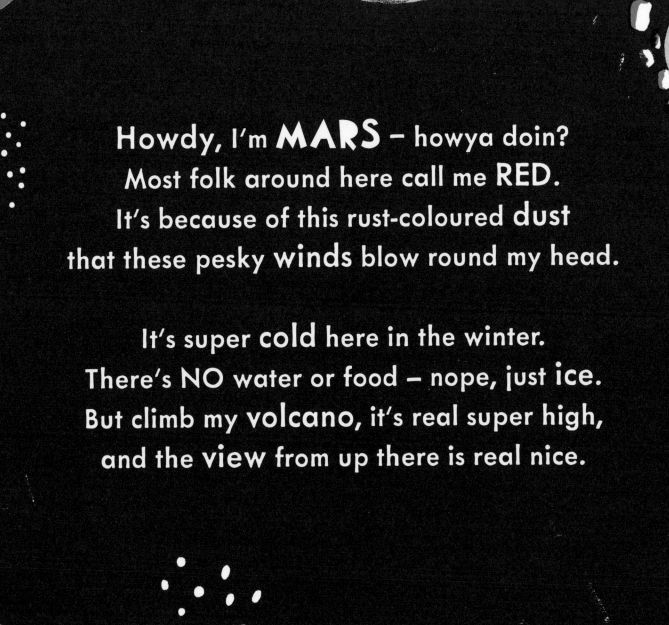

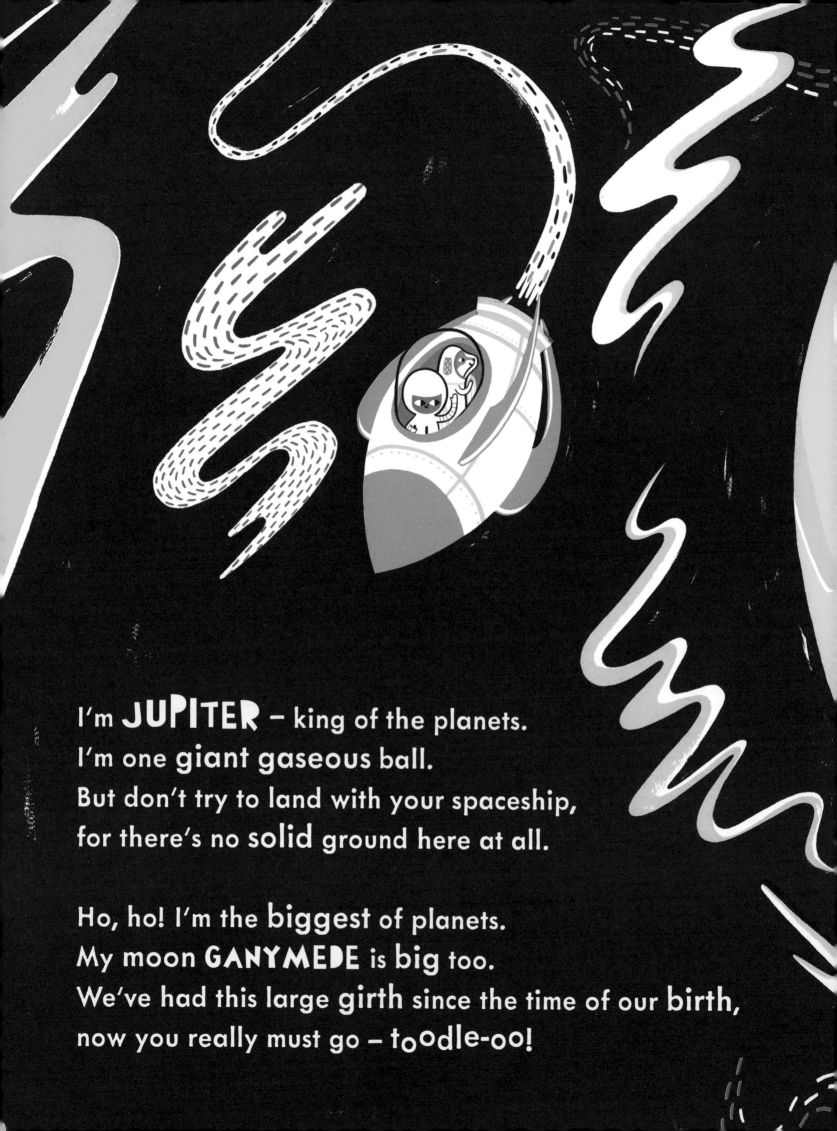

I'm **JUPITER** – king of the planets.
I'm one **giant gaseous ball**.
But don't try to land with your spaceship,
for there's no **solid** ground here at all.

Ho, ho! I'm the **biggest** of planets.
My moon **GANYMEDE** is big too.
We've had this large **girth** since the time of our birth,
now you really must go – **toodle-oo!**

My name's **SATURN** –
oh, don't you just **love** me?
You have to **agree**, I look nice.
Just look at my **RINGS**, aren't they sparkly?
They shimmer with crushed **rock** and **ice**!

You humans can't help but **admire** me.
I'm the **prettiest** planet you've seen.
So be sure to take hundreds of pictures

I'm **URANUS** – golly, I'm f-freezing!
I'm a great swirling windy ice ball.
It's a shame you can't land and **explore** me
but there's **NO rock** in my middle at all!

The name's **NEPTUNE** – *Ice Giant* they call me.
My freezing skies make me look **blue**.
It gets **lonely** out here, all this **way** from the earth,
so I'm mightily pleased to see YOU!

Yoo hoo! It's me! Little **PLUTO** –
I'm a tiny dwarf planet you know.
And, look, this is **CHARON** my buddy,
she's with me wherever I go!

And now it is time to head **homewards** –
back to **EARTH** where our long **journey** ends.
We've had such an **awesome** adventure
and made lots of wonderful **friends**.

So next time that you snuggle down quietly,
look out at the twinkling night sky.
You'll see ALL your friends smiling downwards –
why not give them a wave and shout, "Hi!"?